For SCBWI for providing a place for children's writers to come together, to share, to celebrate. — JRE & SJG

For my father, Roy, my pets: Shawn, Kato, Simone and Martini, the Lucia Kim family, Lilla Rogers and all who have kept me in tune with the universe. — DI

Text copyright © 2000 by Judith Ross Enderle and Stephanie Jacob Gordon.
Illustrations copyright © 2000 by Donna Ingemanson.

The illustrations in this book were rendered with acrylics and oils.
Hand-lettering by Donna Ingemanson.
Book design by Lucy Nielsen. Recipes by Ethel Brennan.
Typeset in Sabon.

Printed in Hong Kong.
ISBN 0-8118-2450-0

Library of Congress Cataloging-in-Publication Data available.

Distributed in Canada by Raincoast Books
8680 Cambie Street, Vancouver, British Columbia V6P 6M9

10 9 8 7 6 5 4 3 2 1

Chronicle Books
85 Second Street, San Francisco, California 94105

www.chroniclebooks.com/Kids

Something's Happening on Calabash Street

by Judith Ross Enderle and Stephanie Jacob Gordon

illustrated by Donna Ingemanson

chronicle books · san francisco

"Mama, what is happening?"

Mischa wants to know.

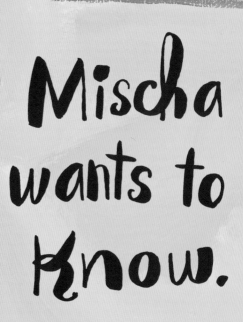

"Soon you'll see, my Mischa.

But now it's time to go."

At the market, neighbors fill baskets
with food for a favorite dish.
The Garcias pick colorful peppers
The Yamaguchis choose a fish.

Mrs. Puccini hums an Opera Song.
In her basket are flour and yeast.

The Dakarais buy a mountain of yams,
Enough for a fantastic feast.

mama chooses cabbages, ROUND as a summer moon.

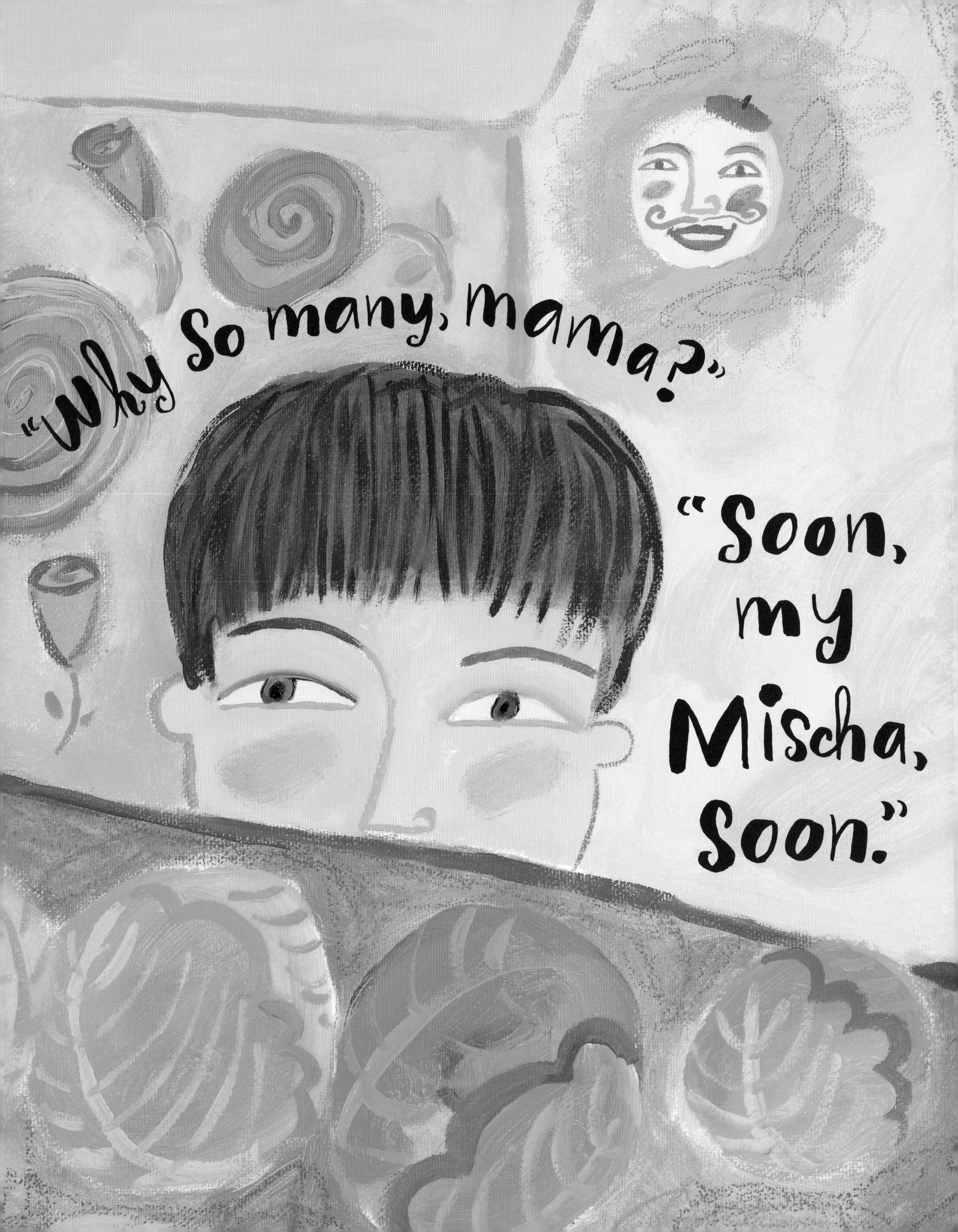

"Why so many, mama?"

"Soon, my Mischa, soon."

Along CALABASH Street
they swing hands
and sing.

The air is Lush with
yummy smells –
Something indeed is happening!

It's then that Mama tells him.
It's then that Mischa Knows.

why the
Trangs bought
Kiwis

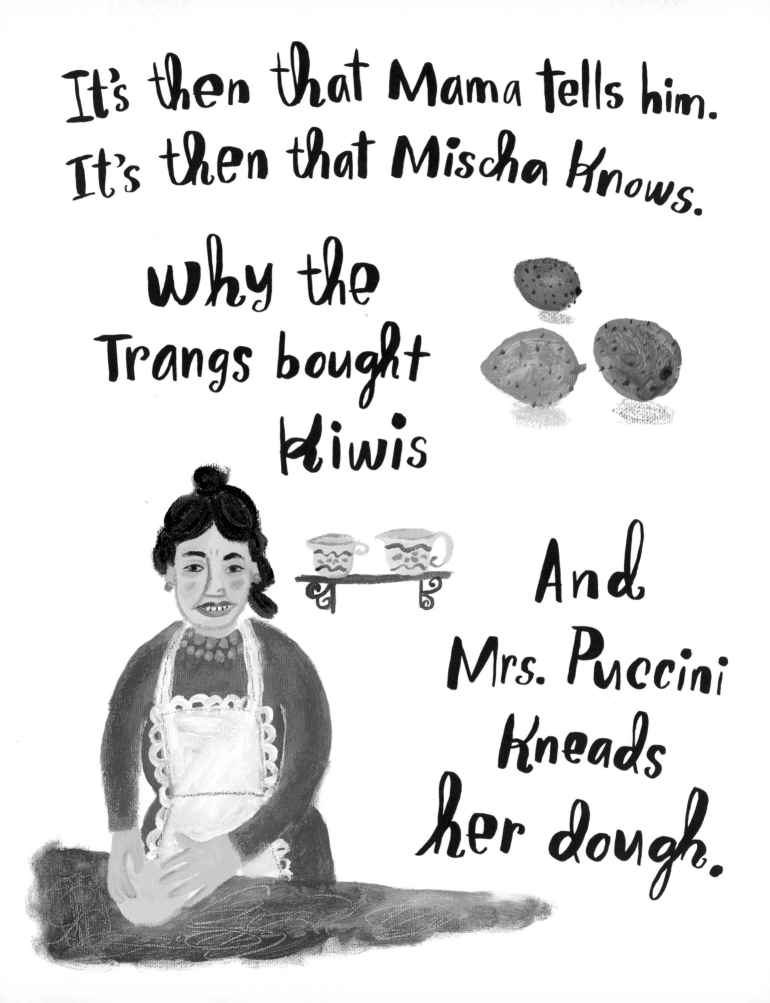

And
Mrs. Puccini
Kneads
her dough.

Why the Lakis roll up grape leaves

And the Choufleurs pour in cream.

why the O'Brien's Stew is bubbling

And the Cohen's Matzo Balls will steam.

why the Harik's rice is Soaking
And the Chambals Stir their curry.

Why the Schultzes make a sweet sauce

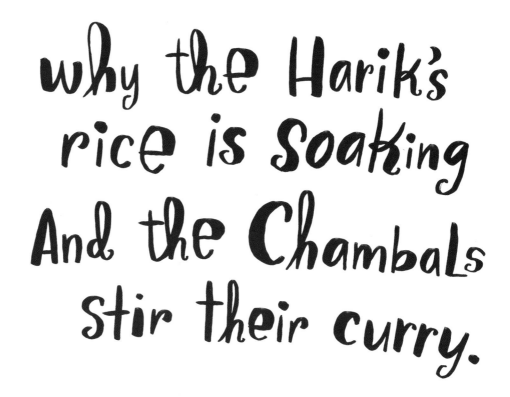

And why Mama and Mischa hurry!

At home, mama boils the water, Mischa adds a pinch of spice.

Baba makes her best Golubtsi — the cabbage is stuffed with meat and rice.

when the sky
grows rosy

Mama's BEst Dish is
covered tight.

Papa carries it proudly,
Mischa Leads the
way Tonight.

Beneath the dancing
lantern light
A steel band bangs
a beat.

Mischa whirls and twirls,
Neighbors wave and greet.

Tables fill with savory dishes,
Mama and Mischa take a seat.

Some of
this and
Some of
that.

It's a fiesta! A gathering! Celebration's in the Air!

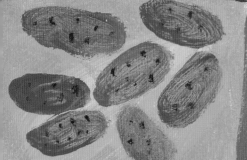

Something's happening on CALAbash Street—
It's the CALABASh Street fair!

IN THE STORY, Mischa helps his family make a favorite dish for a special event. Readers can do the same! Under careful adult supervision, children can help make the foods featured in this book. While the preparation of ingredients such as cutting, chopping, steaming, sautéing and handling of hot liquids should be done by an adult, children will enjoy stirring, whisking, peeling, kneading, rolling and filling, as necessary, for each dish (✋).

The Garcia's Salsa and Corn Chips

The Yamaguchi's Salmon Sushi Rolls

The Lakis' Dolmas

Mrs. Puccini's Mozzarella, Mushroom and Sausage Pizza

The Dakarai's Roasted Yams

The Trang's Tropical Fruit Salad

The Choufleur's Chocolate Truffle Crème

The Cohen's Matzo Ball Soup

The O'Brien's Potato-Apple Stew

The Harik's Saffron Rice

The Chambal's Vegetable Curry

The Schultz's Applesauce

Baba's Golubtsi

The Garcia's Salsa and CORN Chips

12 6-inch-diameter corn tortillas cut into quarters
1/2 red bell pepper, seeds and stem removed, coarsely chopped
1/2 green bell pepper, seeds and stem removed, coarsely chopped
1 tomato, cored and coarsely chopped
1/4 cup sweet red onion, coarsely chopped
2 tablespoons fresh cilantro leaves

Preheat oven to 400° F.

To prepare the chips, arrange the tortilla slices in a single layer on nonstick baking sheets and toast in the oven until crisp, about 5 minutes. When the chips are done, remove from the oven, let them cool and then place in a bowl.

To make the salsa, combine the peppers, tomato, onion and cilantro in a food processor and pulse several times until the ingredients are finely chopped and blended together. Place the salsa in a small bowl and serve with the tortilla chips.

Children can arrange the tortillas on the baking sheets, remove the stems and seeds from the peppers and tear the cilantro leaves from the sprigs.

SERVES 12.

The Yamaguchi's Salmon Sushi Rolls

2/3 pound salmon steak
1 tablespoon soy sauce
1/4 teaspoon freshly ground ginger
1/2 cucumber, peeled, seeds removed and thinly sliced lengthwise
1/2 carrot, peeled, quartered lengthwise then thinly sliced
4 cups cooked quick-sushi rice, prepared according to instructions
4 standard size sheets of dried seaweed

For the dipping sauce:
1/4 cup soy sauce
1 teaspoon wasabi paste (optional)

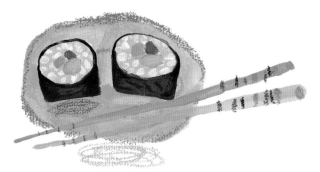

Preheat the broiler.

Place the salmon in a bowl with 1 tablespoon of soy sauce and the ground ginger and turn the fish until well coated. Set aside and let marinate for about 10 minutes. Place the fish on a sheet of aluminum foil and fold up the edges. Cook the fish in the broiler for about 5 minutes, until just golden, and turn, cooking another 5 minutes. The fish should flake easily when done. When the salmon has cooled enough to touch, remove and discard the skin and bones and set aside.

To make the rolls, lightly toast the seaweed over a gas or electric burner by passing it just over the top 2 or 3 times—this will slightly crisp it. Spread about 1 cup of cooked rice over 1 sheet of seaweed to within 1 inch of the edge furthest from you. At the edge nearest to you place 2 strips each of cucumber and carrot and some salmon atop the rice. Gently but firmly roll the seaweed up over the filling away from you, keeping the cucumber, carrots and fish toward the bottom edge. When the roll is finished, brush the edge with water and press gently so the seaweed edge sticks to the roll. Repeat until the 4 rolls are completed. Using a sharp, clean knife, slice the roll crosswise into 1 inch rounds. Make a spicy mixture of wasabi paste and soy sauce or just soy sauce. Beware: wasabi is very strong. Use sparingly.

Children can help fill and roll the rolls.

SERVE IMMEDIATELY. SERVES 6.

the Lakis' Dolmas

3 cups cooked long-grain rice

1/2 cup pine nuts

1/2 cup chopped fresh herbs—cilantro, parsley and dill

1/2 cup fresh-squeezed lemon juice

2 tablespoons olive oil

1/4 teaspoon salt

20 pickled grape leaves

1 cup vegetable broth

Preheat oven to 325° F.

In a large bowl, mix together the rice, pine nuts, chopped herbs, 1/2 of the lemon juice, 1 tablespoon of the olive oil and the salt.

To make the dolmas, unfold a leaf and place about 1 tablespoon of filling on the center of each leaf, fold the stem end over the filling and fold the sides in toward the middle. Roll the stem end up and gently press down on the finished roll with your palm to seal the seam. Repeat this process until the grape leaves are all filled. Oil the sides and bottom of a baking dish large enough to hold the dolmas and layer them in the dish seam sides down. Pour the broth and the remaining olive oil and lemon juice over the dolmas, cover with aluminum foil and bake for 45 minutes.

Once the herbs are chopped and the broth heated, children can fill and roll the dolmas.

MAKES 20 DOLMAS.

Mrs. Puccini's Mozzarella, Mushroom and Sausage Pizza

For the crust:

1 cup warm water (108° F)

1 package (2-1/2 teaspoons) active dry yeast

1 teaspoon sugar

3-1/2 cups all-purpose flour

1 teaspoon salt

6 tablespoons olive oil

1/2 cup cornmeal

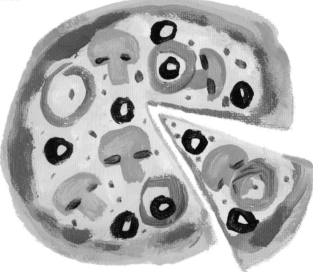

For the sauce:

1 tablespoon olive oil

1 15-ounce can chopped tomatoes

2 sprigs fresh basil

2 teaspoons dried oregano

1 bay leaf

1/4 teaspoon black pepper

1/4 teaspoon salt

For the topping:

4 cups grated mozzarella cheese (about 1 cup per pizza)

2 cups sliced mushrooms (optional)

1/2 pound Italian sausage, bulk or casings removed (optional)

(Use favorite toppings in place of those suggested here.)

To prepare the dough, combine the warm water, yeast and sugar in a small bowl. Let stand until foamy, about 5 minutes.

In a large bowl, combine the flour, salt, 3 tablespoons of olive oil, and the yeast mixture and stir together with a wooden spoon until the ingredients stick together. Transfer the dough to a floured work surface and knead 5 to 7 minutes until smooth and elastic. Form the dough into a ball and coat lightly with about 1 teaspoon of olive oil. Place the ball of dough in the bowl, cover the bowl with a kitchen towel and let rise in a warm place until doubled in size, about 1-1/2 hours.

While the dough is rising, make the tomato sauce. Warm the olive oil over medium heat and add the tomatoes, basil, oregano, bay leaf, pepper and salt and stir to mix well. When the sauce begins to bubble, reduce the heat to low and cover and simmer about 20 minutes. Remove from the heat and set aside.

Preheat oven to 500° F.

This is a hot oven for baking, so adult supervision during cooking is very important. Prepare baking sheets by scattering each with 1 tablespoon of the corn-meal. Punch down the dough and divide into 4 equal portions. On a floured surface, roll out each portion into a round about 10 inches in diameter and 1/8 inch thick. Transfer 1 round to each baking sheet (reserve the other 2 rounds for topping later). Brush the rounds with olive oil and spread about 1/4 cup of sauce evenly over the top to within about 1/2 inch of the edges. Sprinkle about 1/2 cup of the cheese over the sauce, layer 1/2 cup of mushrooms, top with another 1/2 cup of cheese and some sausage. Bake until the cheese begins to bubble, the sausage is cooked through, and the crusts are golden brown, 5 to 7 minutes. When done, transfer the pizzas to a cutting board or a wire rack, cool slightly before slicing, and repeat the process with the remaining 2 dough rounds and toppings.

Children can mix and knead the dough, roll out rounds and top pizzas.

MAKES 4 10-INCH PIZZAS.

The DAKarais' Roasted YAMs

2 tablespoons vegetable oil

1/2 teaspoon salt

1/2 teaspoon pepper

4 large yams cut in halves crosswise and then cut into 1/2-inch-thick wedges

Preheat oven to 450° F.

In a large bowl, combine the oil, salt and pepper, then add the yams, toss to coat well. Arrange wedges on a nonstick baking sheet and bake until they are golden and crisp and can easily be pierced with a fork, about 35 to 40 minutes. Serve hot.

Children can toss the cut yams and arrange them on the baking sheet.

SERVES 4 TO 6.

the Trang's Tropical Fruit Salad

2 coconuts (optional)
4 kiwis
3 soft, ripe mangos
1 honeydew melon
1 tablespoon strained fresh-squeezed lemon juice
1/2 cup shredded coconut

Puncture the coconuts at the three dots located at one end. Turn the coconuts upside down and drain the liquid. Then, on a hard surface, use a hammer to crack the shell with swift hard strokes. When the shell is cracked pull the coconuts apart into halves, creating four bowls.

Peel the kiwis and slice crosswise into 1/4-inch-thick rounds.

Slice the mangos lengthwise along the pit on the wider side of both sides of the fruit. Then cut the remaining strip of flesh from the pit. Make vertical slices about 1/2 inch apart along the flesh side of the mango slices without cutting through the skin. Then do the same crosswise creating 1/2 inch cubes. Invert the flesh so the cubes are separated and cut them from the skin.

Cut the melon into 1 inch cubes.

Combine the kiwis, mangos, melon, lemon juice and shredded coconut in a large bowl, toss and spoon into the halved coconut shells or into a serving bowl. Serve chilled.

Children can peel the kiwis and gently fold the ingredients together.

SERVES 4.

the Choufleur's CHOColate truffle CRÈme

1 cup heavy cream
6 ounces bittersweet chocolate,
   broken into 1 inch pieces
1/4 cup sugar
1 large egg
1 teaspoon vanilla extract
1/4 teaspoon salt

In a large mixing bowl, whip 1/2 cup of the heavy cream to soft peaks and set aside.

In a food processor, fitted with a metal blade, combine the chocolate and the sugar. Pulse until finely ground, then add the egg, vanilla and salt and process until smooth, although small bits of chocolate will remain.

Bring the remaining 1/2 cup of the cream to a boil, stirring constantly. Turn the food processor on and pour in the hot cream in a steady stream and blend until smooth. Then, gently fold the chocolate mixture into the whipped cream until well blended. Transfer the truffle crème to individual 4-ounce ramekins or small desert dishes and chill.

Children can whip the cream and help blend the ingredients.

SERVES 4.

The Cohen's Matzo Ball Soup

For the matzo balls:
6 eggs
1-1/2 teaspoons salt
3/4 cup water
1-1/2 cups matzo meal

For the soup:
4 quarts water
1 onion quartered
3 carrots, 2 cut into halves, 1 diced
3 celery stalks, 2 cut into 2-inch slices,
    1 cut into 1/2-inch slices
4 chicken thighs, skins removed
1 teaspoon salt
1/2 teaspoon pepper
4 sprigs curly leaf parsley
2 bay leaves

Prepare the matzo ball mixture the night before planning to serve the soup. In a mixing bowl, whisk together the eggs. Whisk in the water and then the matzo meal and salt. Cover with plastic wrap and refrigerate overnight.

To make the soup, boil the water and add the onion, carrot halves, celery slices, chicken, salt, pepper, parsley sprigs and bay leaves. Return to a boil and cook uncovered for 40 minutes. Reduce the heat to low, cover and simmer for 30 minutes. Pour the liquid through a colander into a large bowl and return it to the pot. Remove the chicken meat from the bones and add the meat and remaining carrots and celery to the broth and return to a boil. Reduce the heat to low, cover and simmer until the carrots are tender, about 15 minutes.

Bring a large saucepan of water to a boil and add 1 teaspoon of salt. Dampen your fingers and gently make 1 to 2 inch balls with the matzo mixture. When the balls are all made, use a slotted spoon to gently slip the matzo balls into the water.

When they float to the top, reduce the heat to medium, cover and cook for 40 minutes. When done, add the matzo balls to the soup and reheat.

🖐 Children can make the matzo ball batter and form the matzo balls.

SERVES 6.

the O'Brien's Potato-Apple Stew

1 tablespoon olive oil

1/2 small onion, coarsely chopped

2 stalks celery, coarsely chopped

2 cups vegetable broth

2 cups water

3 golden delicious apples, peeled, cored and quartered

2 medium potatoes, peeled and quartered

1/2 teaspoon salt

1/4 teaspoon pepper

1/4 cup heavy cream

In a large saucepan, warm the olive oil over medium heat. Add the onion and celery and sauté until soft, about 5 minutes. Add the vegetable broth and water and bring to a boil. Add the apples, potatoes, salt and pepper and return to a boil. Reduce the heat slightly, cover and continue to cook at a boil for about 10 minutes, reduce the heat and let simmer 20 minutes. The soup is done when the potatoes can easily be pierced with a fork. Transfer the hot soup 1 cup at a time to a blender and puree until smooth. Return the soup to the pot and reheat. Garnish each serving with a teaspoon of cream.

🖐 Once the onions and celery have been sautéed, children can add the ingredients to the soup.

SERVES 4.

The Harik's SAffron Rice

1 tablespoon olive oil
1/4 yellow onion, finely chopped
1 cup Basmati rice
1 teaspoon saffron threads
1/4 cup slivered almonds
1/4 cup raisins
1/4 cup dried apricots, coarsely chopped
1 cinnamon stick
3 cardamom pods, or 1/2 teaspoon ground cardamom
1/4 teaspoon salt
2 cups water

Saffron

Warm the olive oil over medium heat, add the onion and sauté until soft, about 5 minutes, stir in the rice and saffron and cook another minute. Stir in the almonds, raisins, apricots, cinnamon stick, cardamom pods and salt. Pour in the water and bring to a boil, reduce heat to low and cover. Simmer until the liquid has been fully absorbed into the rice, about 20 minutes. Fluff with a fork and serve immediately.

Children can stir the ingredients and fluff the rice just before serving.

SERVES 4.

Cinnamon

CARdamom

The CHambal's Vegetable Curry

1 cup cooked Basmati rice,
    prepared according to package instructions
2 tablespoons vegetable oil
1/2 yellow onion, cut lengthwise into 1/4-inch slices
1 clove garlic, pressed
2 medium potatoes, peeled and cut into 1-inch cubes
2 medium carrots, peeled and cut into 1/2-inch slices
2 teaspoons curry powder
1 red pepper, cut into 1 inch pieces
1 tomato, cored and coarsely chopped
1 cup vegetable broth
1/4 cup golden raisins
1/4 cup plain yogurt
2 teaspoons torn mint leaves

Prepare the rice.

In a large skillet warm the vegetable oil over a medium heat. Add the onion and the garlic and sauté until soft, about 5 minutes. Add the potatoes and carrots and stir. Add the curry powder and stir in the pepper and tomato. Stir often so the mixture does not stick to the skillet. After about 3 minutes add the vegetable broth. Bring the liquid to a boil, reduce the heat to low, add the raisins and cover. Let simmer until the vegetables are cooked through, about 20 minutes.

While the curry is cooking, stir together the yogurt and the chopped mint. Serve the curry over rice and garnish with a spoonful of the yogurt mixture.

Once the vegetables have been chopped and onions and garlic have been prepared, children can stir together ingredients and make the yogurt sauce.

SERVES 4.

the Schultz's APPLesauce

3 pounds apples, peeled and cored
1 cinnamon stick
1 vanilla bean, slit lengthwise, or 1 teaspoon pure vanilla extract
2 cups water
1/4 teaspoon salt

   In a large saucepan with a tight-fitting lid, combine the apples, cinnamon stick, vanilla bean, water and salt and bring to a boil. Reduce the heat to low and let simmer until the apples are very soft and can easily be crushed with the back of a wooden spoon, about 30 minutes. Uncover the saucepan and continue to cook until the liquid is reduced by 1/3.
   Remove the applesauce from the heat, discard the cinnamon stick and mash, or transfer it to a food processor and blend for a smoother sauce. Covered in the refrigerator, it will keep for up to one week.
   Once the apples are cooked down, children can easily mash them with the back of a wooden spoon or a potato masher.

MAKES ABOUT 3 CUPS.

Baba's Golubtsi

1 large green cabbage (about 2 pounds),
   core removed but leaves intact
2 tablespoons olive oil
1 yellow onion, finely chopped
1 pound lean ground beef, crumbled
1/4 teaspoon pepper
1/4 teaspoon ground coriander
1/4 teaspoon salt
1/2 cup cooked long grain rice
1 cup chicken or vegetable broth
1 15-ounce can chopped tomatoes

Preheat oven to 350° F.

Place the cabbage in a large soup pot, fill about 2/3 full with water and bring to a boil. Cover and cook until the leaves begin to separate from the head, about 15 minutes. When the cabbage is done, remove it from the hot water, and let drain in a colander until cool enough to handle. Gently remove 10 leaves from the cabbage and set aside.

Meanwhile, warm the olive oil in a large skillet over medium heat. Add the onion and sauté until soft, about 5 minutes, add the beef and cook another 5 minutes. Use a soupspoon to remove any excess fat that appears as the meat cooks. Add the pepper, coriander, salt and the rice. Cook, stirring occasionally, until the meat is cooked through, about 15 minutes.

To make the stuffed cabbage rolls, place a cabbage leaf on a work surface so that it creates a bowl. Place about 3 tablespoons of the filling in the center of the leaf and fold the bottom edge up over the filling. Fold each side in over the filling and roll the leaf from the bottom up, keeping the filling tight at the bottom end of the roll. Repeat until the filling is used up, about 10 rolls. Arrange the rolls snugly, seam sides down in a deep baking dish with a tight-fitting lid. Pour in the vegetable broth and tomatoes. Cover and bake for 30 minutes and serve hot.

Once the filling is prepared, children can stuff the cabbage.

SERVES 5 TO 6.